AF496618

A practical guidebook to monsters.

Everything you need to know about monsters.

By Ursula Cisa & Max Prendergast.

A practical guidebook to monsters.

Everything you need to know about monsters.

"To Max with all my love."

This book belongs to

____

Max has no magic powers

He is not a superhero. He is just a regular boy.

However, he has a secret weapon, and he

knows everything about monsters.

Max knows that

there are monsters of all sizes. Big, medium,

and small.

Even so, the smallest monsters are 1000 times bigger than any person.

There are all kinds. Some have sharp teeth.
Others are very hairy, have claws and long
tails. Or short.

They feed on people's fear.

They come from different realms and strange places.

They like to come to our world on vacation.

They know how to hide very well. So only a few people have ever seen them. The reason is that monsters, like choosing one person, usually a kid. They start scaring that kid and that kid only, so they hide from everyone else.

They enjoy it so much, so…when you least expect it, the monster roars, leaving you in terror.

They love doing it, so they laugh.
And laughing makes them bigger and
stronger, the same way fear does.

Not even the police can stop them.
The monsters laugh at them too and become
even more powerful.

Max knows all about this because one day, a

monster came into his life.

Then, it began scaring Max.

Every time it did, Max jumped 100 feet high.

The monster would not leave him alone.

It was so annoying.

He tried to ignore it, but it didn't work.

Max tried to tell others about the monster, but

nobody believed him.

The monster kept getting stronger.

Max tried to ignore it again, but it still did not work.

He knew he had to do something.

So, he came up with a plan.

When the monster appeared next, Max's plan
was to scream at the top of his lungs, so
everyone would come running and see the
monster.
It did not work. The monster got a fright and
got the hiccups.
Max laughed out loud.

Max's laughing made the monster smaller and weaker, so it fell into a hole in the floor.

By the time everyone arrived, the monster had escaped through a tunnel. All anyone saw was Max laughing. They thought he was being naughty.

Max became sad. He tried to explain, but nobody listened, and they left.

The monster appeared once again, laughing away, it grew even bigger than before. Max ran as fast as he could and hid.

He wished he could show the monster to everyone, but he understood that it was pointless. All he really wanted was to get rid of it for once and for all. He didn't know what to do.

Suddenly, Max remembered how the monster got frightened and how it shrank when he laughed. Then Max had another idea.

What if he started to laugh at the monster?

So, he made another plan.

Max hid and waited. When the monster
appeared, he laughed as hard as he could.

That gave the monster a good scare.

It was working.

Max kept laughing, and the monster kept shrinking.

It became so small that Max could barely see
him.

Suddenly, it disappeared completely.
It worked! Max was right. Laughing at the
monster made it small and weak and
eventually disappear.
Max could not be happier. His plan had
worked, and the monster was finally gone!

So, that's how Max discovered how to get rid
of monsters.

Now you know everything you need to know
about monsters.

If you ever meet one of them, you do not need
to have magic powers or to be a superhero.

All you need is your secret weapon...

... laughter.

The end.

Published by www.galwayplaytherapy.ie

About the Author

Ursula Cisa is a Therapeutic Play Practitioner graduated from the National University of Ireland Galway (NUIG) and the Academy of Play and Child Psychotherapy (APAC).

She is a member of Play Therapy Ireland and Play Therapy International.

She is also the author of "Marvin the little happy dragon" and "Castor wants to help".

This story was inspired and illustrated by Max Prendergast's drawings.

Marvin, the happy little dragon

Marvin is a little dragon with a big problem. He can't control his fire. Can he learn how?

Castor wants to help

Every morning the dam floods. A small beaver decides to take charge and stop the floods.

Printed in Poland
by Amazon Fulfillment
Poland Sp. z o.o., Wrocław